WEEKLY READER
CHILDREN'S BOOK CLUB
presents

GIANT JOHN

BY ARNOLD LOBEL

HARPER & ROW, PUBLISHERS
NEW YORK, EVANSTON, AND LONDON

for Gale

Long ago in an enchanted forest
there lived a large giant named John.

The fairies, who also lived
in the forest, played magic
dancing music for John.
He had to dance and dance
and could not stop until
the music stopped.
The dancing made John's big feet hurt,
but he thought it was great fun.

In the evening he would pick a bouquet of trees
and take them home to his mother.
One night his mother began to cry.
"We are poor," sobbed Mrs. Giant.
"There are only two potato chips in the cupboard,
and we have no money to buy more food."

After they ate the potato chips, John said,
"Do not cry, Mother. Soon we will have
some money. I will go out into the world
to find a job."
Mrs. Giant made John wear his rubbers
and carry his umbrella.
"Good-bye, Mother," said John as he
started on his journey.

John walked very far out into the world.
He saw mountains and tigers and thunderstorms.
He saw a beautiful castle.

"Look, look," cried the king
and queen and princess and dog,
who lived in the castle.
"Here comes a giant!"
"Hello," called John,
"I am looking for a job."

"Stay awhile and work for us," said the king.
John liked the king and queen and princess and dog.
He decided to stay and went right to work.

When it rained, he kept the castle dry.

And when it was sunny and hot, he blew a pleasant breeze.

He helped the queen do the laundry

and played horsey to make the dog and princess laugh.

John cleaned and dusted
the castle every day.

The king and queen and princess and dog
were very happy.
They did not even mind when John's snoring
kept them awake at night.

On Saturday the king gave John a big bag of gold
for all the work he had done.
"We'll have a picnic lunch before you go home,"
said the queen.
Suddenly a cloud of fairies appeared.
They were John's friends from the enchanted forest.
"We missed you, Giant John," they said.
"There is no one to dance to our magic music.
We came to play for you."

The fairies began to play the magic dancing music.
John began to dance.

"Ouch!" said the king
and queen and princess and dog
as they fell to the ground.
"Stop, stop!" shouted John,
but the fairies kept playing their music
and John danced and danced.

John could not stop dancing.
He danced everywhere.
He danced on the flowers
and on the dog's tail.

He danced on the castle.
"You foolish fairies," cried John.
"Stop that terrible music!"

The fairies did stop their music.
They saw what they had done and were very sorry.
The king and queen and princess and dog
were all crying.

But Giant John did not cry.
He began to put the castle
back together again.
The fairies helped too.
They bandaged the flowers
and the dog's tail.

John worked hard,
and soon the castle was fixed.
It did not look quite the same
as before, but the king
and queen and princess and dog
dried their eyes
and thought it was beautiful.

"Now I must go home," said John, putting on his
rubbers and hat. He promised to visit often and
kissed the king and queen and princess and dog good-bye.

John rushed home to his mother
with the bag of gold.
"Look, Mother," he called,
"I have earned some money for us."

By this time Mrs. Giant was very, very hungry.
She was glad to see John and his bag of gold
coming through the door.

That night John and his mother invited the fairies to dinner.
They did not dance, but they ate baked beans
and sang many songs and lived happily ever after.